Ghost Dick

Special Thanks:

Jen and Ian. True patrons of the arts. And also crap like this.

When the dame walked into my office, the first thing I noticed was her legs went all the way up to the top of where legs go. Which is good. I'd just had a thing with a woman with a bionic leg. And the thing we had was that I spilled soda on her bionic leg, and then her bionic leg stopped working and she used her regular leg to kick the shit out of me.

The second thing I noticed about the dame in my office was that her legs also went all the way down to the floor. Another good sign. I had a thing with that lady who invented hover shoes. That didn't work out either because I kept "accidentally" getting us into situations that required her to hover us across a lake or a swamp or some water on her hover shoes while I rode piggyback. You can only get away with that so many times with the inventor of hover shoes before she realizes you're using her for her hover shoes. And that amount of times is three, so enjoy them.

Something that's weird about me, normally-smart women, like ones who invent hover things, seem to come my way every so often.

Something that's not weird about me is that I'm a paranormal investigator. Which is a fancy way to say ghost detective.

Wait, I guess that's weird too.

Okay, the not weird thing is, this dame came in and there was nothing unusual about her legs.

So this dame with the regular kind of legs came into my office, which is a table at Burger King. I picked this particular Burger King for my office because two reasons:

1. More than once I've seen someone passed out in the bushes outside, and when that's going on, someone who is quietly using a table as a ghost detecting office doesn't really make the list of priorities.

2. They have free wifi. I don't own a computer, so that doesn't really matter to me, but if I ever did get a computer I wouldn't want to relocate. It's always good to plan for business growth.

3. They have chicken rods. I know I said it was only two reasons, but the chicken rods are meaningful to me. Just as a

note, Burger King DOES NOT like when you call them chicken "rods."

The dame sat down, and I swallowed hard. It was time to look at her face or her torso or some part of her besides her legs. Hopefully none of her other parts was hovering or mechanical or anything else.

I should also mention, part of what made it so hard to tear my eyes away from her legs was because she didn't have any pants on. I probably should have said that earlier. I'm a pretty good investigator, but the part I'm worst at is when the investigation is over and you have to tell everything that happened. That part I suck at. Which is ALL this book is, so buckle up because you're in for a confusing ride with a drunk driver.

And also buckle up because if you're reading this in a car, you should definitely use a seatbelt. You're almost certainly going to crash if you read and drive.

I looked at the rest of the woman who sat in the chair across from me, and it wasn't just her legs that went all the way up. Her eyelashes went all the way up to her eyes, her arms went all the way up to her torso. Everything about her began and ended at the spot where it was supposed to.

I was pretty sure I was in love.

She said, "Are you the guy?"

I said, "The guy?"

She said, "The investigator. The—" and she leaned in closer, "ghost investigator."

I said, "That's me. Did you know you're not wearing any pants?"

She said, "Good observational skills. That's a start."

I smiled, pleased with myself. That was exactly what I was hoping she'd say. "Takes a detective to spot one," I said.

She said, "I'm having a problem with a succubus."

And then I rolled my eyes.

If you ever get in the paranormal investigation game, what you'll find out right away is that the favorite way people like to screw over their husband or their wife is to lie about a succubus. It never fails. Someone says their wife is a succubus, you go to look, and it turns out that the woman is just your run of the mill asshole. Which is bad, but not paranormal. You fire a couple warning shots at center mass, which should only mildly annoy a succubus, and all of a sudden you shot this human woman a bunch of times. If you're lucky like me, the woman you shoot turns into this big rapper and tells everyone that she got shot on the streets and pays you some money to never tell the story about how what really happened is a dum-dum thought she was a ghost.

I said, "Tell me a little bit about what this succubus is doing."

She said, "The succubus is coming into our bedroom almost every night. She sleeps with my husband."

"Do you mean she sexes on him or that he sleeps next to him?"

I say stuff like "sexes" because I can pretend it's a technical term for ghost sex and show my authority. Plus, I fuck up words all the time, but if you hide your fuckups behind a bunch of on purpose stuff, people stop asking and figure that if they call you on it, you'll have this long explanation that sounds like total bullshit (and it is), but who wants to sit through another explanation? Explanations are the worst because no one ever explains to you about how smart you are or that you're right. It's always like "And that's why you're wrong and a dumb idiot."

She said, "They have sex. Definitely."

I said, "How do you know?" and I take out a pad of paper. A yellow one. That's a legal pad, and people who want to think you're a real detective definitely want to see you take out something with the word legal on it. It's calming. Especially when you're doing something that's not very legal at all.

She says, "Because I watch them do it."

I say, "What do you mean? Like you see the whole thing? The whole act?"

She says, "Yes."

And I say, "You can see the succubus' entire body and everything?"

"Yes, she says."

I say, "Is she like a 8 or better? Let's investigate tonight."

The woman took me to her house. It looked like a haunted house. Except for it was a new townhouse and there were lots of lights on and there was a donut shop across the way, so the whole place smelled like cinnamon donuts. Not a very haunted smell. The whole thing was really pleasant, to be honest. I guess something just seemed weird. Maybe the Halloween decorations all over the goddamn place. Especially the fake spider webs, which I hate because it's so hard to tell which ones are real and which ones are fake. "Real" and "fake" are just words that don't really explain the important differences between a bunch of insulation fibers that probably make you have tumors and threads that come out of a spider's ass. I'm told webs aren't spider shit, but I'm not buying it. Show me a log of spider shit, then I'll believe you.

I follow the lady around to the side of her house. I hate going to houses. They're always nicer than my place. Take this lady's house. The gate to her backyard actually works. Every place I've ever lived with a gate, it's all fucked up. It drags on the ground or you have to break it kind of, or someone left a mean dog back there because it's not your house, it's the neighbors house, but who can tell the difference when you're drunk and it's late and your normal way to know your house is "It's the one with the broken gate"?

Or take the bushes outside this lady's house, they're different from all the bushes in places where I lived. The bushes at this lady's house aren't all full of Cheetos bags.

It's just depressing to go to somewhere that people live and they actually care about it. It's like, stop rubbing it in my face that your bushes aren't all full of snack bags (ALWAYS empty) and that where you live everyone's legs aren't all dog bit.

"Are you crying?" the lady says.

I wipe my eyes on my sleeve and then I wipe my sleeve on the side of her house, and I say no because that's what you have to say when someone asks you that.

She says, "Well, whatever. Just stop moaning so loud. My husband will hear you if you keep it up."

I say, "Okay. I'll try. Do you have anything I can put in my mouth? At home when I'm not crying like this, I put a blanket or the end of a pistol or something in my mouth."

She says, "You're weird."

I say, "It's soothing. I'm not going to bother describing it to you. Seems like you're just going to be closed-minded about it."

We wait silently. Mostly silently. I see how in the bedroom there's sheets and pillow cases that match and don't have Spider-Man on them, and I jam most of my fist in my mouth.

We wait what feels like forever, long enough that the lady gets over her revulsion and rubs my back to try and calm me down until I close my eyes and accidentally say, "Thanks, mom." She stops then. Which makes sense.

And then the succubus shows up.

"That's her," the lady says.

"No shit," I say. "It's a naked girl mounting your husband."

It was kinda mean. But the shortest path to feeling better is putting someone else down. Don't let anyone tell you otherwise. They just want to save all the good slams for themselves.

The lady says, "So? Can you exorcise it or whatever?"

I said, "Oh totally. But we should let them finish. If you interrupt the ritual it gets all fucked up. In the demon realm."

It took about three seconds to figure out that the succubus was just the regular kind of lady dressed up in weird clothes and with flour or something all over her. But she was pretty good looking and so was the husband, so I thought we might as well see how this played out.

The husband pulled out and finished on the succubus' face. I don't know if that's important to the story or not. When you're a detective, all the information is kind of important, but maybe it's not all that important to tell you about it. But I guess I already told you this dude hosed the fake succubus' face, so whatever. It's out there now, and like they say, you can't put the toothpaste back in the tube. Which I always assumed meant you can't put the cum back in the dick. Which I've found to be *very* true.

After the cum part (see earlier description for more details), the succubus got up and left. I told the lady, "Wait here," and I walked around the house and met the succubus at the front door.

"Hey," I said.

She was surprised to see me, and she was all, "Oh, uh, oooooooo. I'm a suuuuckibus."

"Okay," I said. "That's enough. Look, I don't want to blow up your spot here, but this guy's wife is paying me to ghost bust you."

She looked down and thought about it, and then she said, "Oooo-"

And I said, "Stop, okay? I know you're not a succubus."

She said, "How do you know?"

And I said, "Well, for one thing, when you tell a real succubus they're not a succubus, all these tentacles come out or they do some ghosty shit and walk through a wall. They don't ask how you knew."

She slumped a little bit and I said, "Also, a succubus always has good posture. Because their bodies don't have actual weight, see."

"Finally," I said, "Occam's Razor."

She looked up and squinted at me. She said, "Occam's razor? What do you mean, Occam's Razor?"

She had me there. Most times if you say "Occam's Razor" people just sort of give up and nod.

I said, "Why don't you tell me what you think it means and I'll tell you if you're close to the right answer?"

"That's dumb. You're dumb," she said.

She had me there. "Alright, fine. But still. I know you're real because," and then I shoved her down on the sidewalk.

"Hey," she said. "That hurt."

If you're losing a debate and someone is about to prove you're stupid, I really recommend you shove them down. It's way harder to argue when you're on the ground and your ass hurts.

I said, "Can you just fuck this guy not in his house with his wife next to him?"

She said, "But…this works for us."

I said, "I'm not even asking you to stop banging a married man on a nightly basis. I'm just asking you to stop banging him in the same bed where he sleeps with his wife while the wife is in the bed and you're pretending to be supernatural. I feel like I'm not asking for very much here."

She thought about that.

"Plus," I said, "If you say no, I'll push you down again. I might not know Occam's Razor, but I know Mike's Shove, and I'll show you how Mike's Shove works as many times as it takes to make you stop pretending to be a ghost."

She rolled her eyes. I said, "I'm Mike, by the way. It's my shove. That's how I know it."

She said, "I'm calling the police."

She pulled out her phone. I screamed "Occam's Razor!" and slapped the phone out of her hand. I said, "I'm charging this lady $80 bucks. I'll give you $30, and all you have to do is meet this guy out in his car and bang him there."

Here's the thing about being a paranormal detective: you're mostly regular detective. Mostly, you just see exactly what some guy's wife sees, but you don't care, so you can see that the truth is everyone is just making up a ghost story so they don't have to face reality.

Occam's Razor? You tell me.

Don't tell anyone this part, but I don't have my complete, totally finished ghost detective license yet. I'm really close. Just a couple more classes. But if people knew that I wasn't a complete, whole, legitimate paranormal investigator, they'd flip. Can you imagine? If someone found out I wasn't certified? Me? Mike? That's the kind of scandal that could bring the whole ghost detection industry to its knees.

The class I'm in right now is about capturing sounds during a haunting. We use these big microphones that kind of look like dicks, and we plug them into these recorders that also look like dicks. The microphones looking like dicks makes sense to me because a lot of microphones sort of look like dicks. But why the recorders look like dicks, that part I'm not sure about. It might be another test to see if we're ready to be ghost detectives. If we're mature enough that when we see something that looks like a dick, we don't have to run around and tell everyone about it.

Our class met at an abandoned factory for our final. We were supposed to go in there, record some sounds, and then edit the tapes to show if there were any ghost noises.

I got partnered up with the the worst guy in the class. His name is Vance, and he's this hardcore ghost guy. He always wears a short sleeve black shirt that's so tight you can see all his muscles. Which sounds okay, but I can see the outline of his belly button too, which also has muscles. I don't think most people have muscles on their belly button. Mine's just a hole.

Somehow, seeing a belly button muscle through a shirt is worse than seeing it regular. Like how it works with nipple rings. Which Vance also has.

We go into the factory, and Vance hands me all the recording gear, and he starts doing this thing he does all the time. He has this method he worked up that's really annoying. He calls it "going aggro," and how it works is he yells at the ghosts to make them come out.

"Come at me, bro!" he yells. "I ain't afraid of no ghosts!"

When he yells, he throws his arms up so you can see that the muscles in his arms are really big. There's a way you can put up your arms that's regular, and there's a way that's to prove you have big muscles. Vance does it the big muscles way all the time.

He looks over at me to yell something too. This is why I hate being partners with Vance. It's hard to think of something that sounds good to yell. And I sound stupid when I yell at ghosts because I'm not a very good yeller. And all of this is being recorded on my ghost microphone, so it has to be good.

"Any ghosts in here are...toast," I say. Not the best. But it rhymed at least.

Vance sticks out his bottom lip, nods his head. I never get looks where someone tells me I did a good job, so I just have to guess that's what's going on here.

We walk around in the factory for a while, and I hold the microphone out in front of me while Vance yells. I yell a couple other things, and then Vance says, "You know, rhymes aren't tough or cool. They're just...rhymes."

I wanted to say something about how lots of rappers are tough and THEY rhyme. But instead I just shut up and try to record ghosts some more.

I don't know what it is about haunted factories, but there's a few things they ALWAYS have inside.

They always have mannequins inside. A mannequin room, a closet stuffed with mannequins with no heads. Even places that don't have any use for a mannequin, like a yo-yo factory, you'll find one. If you ask the people who used to run the place, they'll tell you the boss at the factory used to hang his suit coats on a mannequin to try and make his clothes keep shape or something like that. And then you knock over the mannequin on accident and it turns out that it's the preserved torso of the boss' missing wife that he mounted on a pole and dressed up and slow danced with, and it's a pretty safe bet that this torso mannequin is why there's a ghost running around in the factory saying stuff like, "OooooOOOOoo," and, "I'm a ghoooOOOoost," and "My torso is in in my husband's OOOooooOfice!"

They don't always say that last one. I wish they did. It would be a lot easier if they could just say what the fuck they wanted. Instead, you walk around until you knock over the mannequin, like I said before, and then you get a good scare. And also it stinks really bad and believe me, when you knock over an old torso, you throw those clothes away. Even your underwear reeks.

But there's an important lesson: Sometimes you solve a ghost case by just being clumsy as hell. That's how I do it, anyway. People will make fun of you for tripping and falling into the answer all the time, like it's so easy. You try falling on top of a preserved old woman corpse that bursts open with juices like an old bag of garbage from a slaughterhouse. You do that and tell me how easy it is, smart guy.

Another thing these old factories always have is some kind of weird machine. A machine where someone who worked there, they'll be like, "Oh, that's designed to screw caps on soda bottles." But then you look at it and it's got crazy drills and killing machine parts and a reservoir filled with virgin's blood. And everyone is all surprised when the machine kills someone. Well, maybe if you didn't put a bunch of weird knives and lasers on a machine that absolutely didn't need them, you'd be a lot safer.

The other thing these old factories always have is a bathroom. It's not always spooky. Most times it isn't. Most ghosts will tell you that scaring someone while they poop is low-hanging fruit. Plus, they might be ghosts, but they don't want to see someone stand up and make a run for it mid-log. Even if you're a ghost and you're all gorey and stuff, there's some stuff that's still gross. It's one thing to be into floating around with your arm chopped off or having blood come out of your mouth. It's another thing to see someone with a hot poop smeared all over their ass.

I'm not telling you about the bathroom because it's somewhere you need to check out for ghosts or something. I'm telling you about it because when you go on these things, if you're like me, you'll probably have to take a pee at some point. And by "if you're like me" I mean "if you're like a human being who consumes liquid and then pees it out." Because you'll always end up drinking a lot of coffee so you can stay up until really late and record ghosts. And it's best practice to try not hold in pee because there's a chance that very same pee will get scared out of you. I always say, "Peeing while you're calm-headed is always better than peeing when you're panicked. Mostly because when you're panicked and peeing, your pants and underwear are still on. And your socks. And if you don't know why I'm mentioning socks, you've never REALLY hosed in your own pants before."

I say that all the time, but I wish there was a better way to say it that wasn't so many words and was maybe catchier and would fit better on a t-shirt or something. I tried "Keep Calm and Pee On," but by the time I caught onto that whole "Keep Calm" trend it was pretty much over. There were really old and slobby people wearing shirts that said "Keep Calm and" and then the rest of the shirt would say something about how it's funny to be old or to fart, or sometimes a shirt would say "Keep Calm" and then something that I bet Cathy said in that comic strip she was in. Which was called *Cathy.* And I hate it.

Vance was yelling something to this big open room about how ghosts probably can't even bench three-thousand pounds or something (I can't remember the amount of pounds he said and I have no idea what's a good amount of pounds to bench press), and I told him, "I'm gonna go find the bathroom."

"Good idea," he said. "Probably lots of ghosts in there."

I said, "Yeah, probably."

Vance said, "Me? I never go in the bathroom. Don't have to." And then he patted his hip. I didn't know what it meant, and then he patted his butt. I didn't know what that meant either, so I followed his lead and patted my stomach.

He said, "No, man. Diapers." He grabbed a piece of his crotch, and I heard a crackling sound. "I wear these bad boys so I can piss and crap myself and I don't have to worry about missing out on confronting a ghost just because of a little pee."

I said, "That's really hardcore." That seemed to satisfy him, and he went back to yelling around.

I don't know if wearing a diaper is really hardcore or if it's just stupid. But it probably doesn't matter. Something can be stupid AND hardcore. Most hardcore things are also stupid.

It's just that hardcore people are too nuts and too scary to call stupid.

When I found the bathroom, there was a men's and a women's. I picked the women's first, and when I took one step inside there was a raccoon in there, and it was howling and giving birth. Right there on the floor of the bathroom, in the middle of this nest of garbage and paper towels and stuff. It was one of those things that's so gross and also beautiful, but then when you really think about it, it's only gross. It's not really beautiful at all. I don't think there's such a thing as being so gross it's beautiful. That's what they say about someone like a really hot model who has one crooked tooth or something. Her body and face and everything are a 10, but she's got this one crooked tooth, and we're like, "Oh, she's even MORE beautiful because she's flawed." No way, man. I'd still tolerate a sexing with her if they straightened out that tooth. You would too.

Trust me, watching a baby raccoon emerge from inside the mom, it's pure disgust-o. And baby raccoons make these weird noises, like birds that got hit by a bus.

I decided to go ahead and switch to the men's room and hope there wasn't something in there giving birth, or at least if there was, it was less gross. If that didn't work out and I had to take my chances with the raccoon again, maybe by the time I got back the raccoon would be done and the babies would be cute like baby animals are supposed to be.

The men's room was empty other than three stalls and a trough to pee in.

I don't know if everyone's seen the trough. That seems to be going out of style. And calling it a trough doesn't help because how many people hang out around horses and troughs and shit like that anymore? It's like me comparing something to, I don't know, a wagon wheel or something. Who has wagon wheel experience anymore?

The trough is like...imagine a long, skinny bathtub, and then it's stuck up on the wall at waist height. And you can take a piss in there. Which might make it even more like your bathtub, depending on how often you pee in it.

The good news is you can fit a lot of people at a trough. But when you feel the mist of the backsplashing pee from someone else, that's when you figure out the problem with the trough. Or when someone's arm is brushing up against you. Think it's annoying when you're on an airplane and sort of fighting for the armrest? Imagine doing that except you and the other person have your stuff all out and you're pissing and feeling the splash from each others' pisses. The trough is the only place this is acceptable. If you started peeing on the person you were fighting for the armrest with on the airplane, there would be some serious issues. Take my word on that one. It's the word of experience.

But having the whole trough to myself, that was a different story. That was like having the whole row on the airplane to yourself. You can pee on whatever seats you want!

I set the recording stuff down on the edge of the sink, and I walked over to the trough. It was full of a bunch of old building stuff, but underneath the pipes were still hooked up.

That's a good thing to check for. Sometimes in these old buildings, they'll have a place to piss and then while you go, you hear this sound that's a whole lot like the piss is going straight on the floor, and your shoes get all covered in piss.

I started on one side of the trough, and then walked towards the other side. I took tiny steps and made click-clack typewriter sounds with every step, and when I got to the right side of the trough, I said DING and ran back to the left side of the trough, peeing the whole time.

You're probably thinking that there's way too much detail in here about me peeing. And you're right. And you're wrong. See, it's not about the piss and the typewriter piss. It's about when I finished, and then I said, "And then they lived happily ever after" and I zipped up my pants, and I turned around and there was a ghost.

There are times in your life when you do something embarrassing, and it's even worse because you get caught doing that thing.

For me, there's a lot of those times. They happen most of the time I do anything, so you'd think I'd stop doing embarrassing things. But it doesn't help. I crap with the door open and sing a song and that's when someone walks in, or I pull my car way too far forward and it scrapes on the curb right when my blind date shows up at the restaurant, and she's standing right there and sees the whole thing. And you panic and step on the gas again, and you run over the lady you were about to go on a date with. And then when you're on trial for murdering her, you get away with it mostly because you hadn't met her yet, and her sister is there and says how she believes you and the dead lady never met because there's no way her dead sister would date a moron like that. And it's good you don't go to jail, but the bad part is that the lady you were meeting for the date sounds like she would have been a really fun person to date, but now she's dead because you ran her over with her car. It's really embarrassing.

That's how things went with the ghost after I turned around and figured he saw me do the whole typewriter peeing thing at the trough.

I said, "I hope you're not expecting me to pee my pants. I just went."

The ghost just floated there. He didn't say anything. I couldn't tell for sure if he was a dude at first, but I guessed because he WAS in the men's room. But maybe the ghost just saw the raccoon in the women's bathroom.

And I guess I should tell you what the ghost looked like. That's what everyone wants to know.

It looked like a ghost. A regular ghost. Something people don't know is that most ghosts look like the way you think ghosts look from TV and stuff, but really crappy TV. Not a good show that's on a network that has mostly terrible shows and has one surprise hit show, but nobody really knows it's a hit until way after it's over. The ghosts look like ghosts from the regular kind of show, the kind that doesn't have a lot of money for a ghost wardrobe budget so they just put someone in a white sheet and put black eye holes on it and that's pretty much it.

Most ghosts look like a white sheet with eye holes.

I don't always tell people that. Because they think it's dumb. But it's true. Why do you think someone decided that's what ghosts look like in the first place? Just by chance? How the hell would you make that up in your head? Wouldn't everyone who saw it be like, "That's dumb. Can't it be scarier?"

I'm here to tell you that cheap Halloween decorations got it right. Real witches, they're weird old crones with warty noses and stuff. The devil is a red guy with a goatee (I met him once, or a guy I was pretty sure was him. But that's a story for another time, and also one I'm not really supposed to tell. But let's just say it involved a fiddling contest in the southern United States that I saw because I got lost in my car and ended up watching this guy have a fiddle contest with the devil. And the guy was pretty good, but the devil was better, to be honest. But then when it was time to vote on who won, everyone got all pissed off because I said the devil definitely won. And they were all like, "That guy is going to lose his soul if he loses this contest!" And I said, "Well, nobody told me that." Anyway, I guess I said I wasn't going to tell you about the devil, but then I did. Damn it).

Because the ghost hadn't made any noise yet, I said, "If it's okay with you, I'm going to cross the room and pick up my machine over here."

They tell you in paranormal investigation school that you should tell a ghost what you're doing every step of the way so you don't surprise them. That way they won't get mad at you.

I stepped sideways, and I held my hands up. I don't know why. Maybe I just got a vibe that the ghost used to be a police guy or something.

When I got to my recorder, I saw the red light was on and I'd never turned it off. Which was great because that meant my typewriter pee was on this tape, and all I could think about was how I was going to have this proof there was a ghost and it'd be on the same tape as me inventing a novelty way to pee when you're at a trough and no one else is there.

But I had to put that aside. This was for the greater good.

I said, "I'm going to talk to you, and if you want to talk, please do, and I'll listen."

This is something else they told us to do in paranormal investigator school. And it's an idea I adopted in my whole life. When I meet up with someone, I just start talking until they try to get in. And even then I might try and shut them out if what they're saying isn't as important as what I'm saying. Hey, I did all the hard work of getting this conversation started, and now all of a sudden you want to horn in on it? Go fuck yourself, buddy.

The ghost hovered, but it didn't say anything.

"So," I said. "Some stuff you should know about me right away. I did suffer multiple head injuries in elementary school. Most were my own fault. All of them were my own fault depending on your point of view. You know those nets that go on the ceiling and you can put stuffed animals in them? I had one of those, but I put a rock collection in there, and, anyway, I don't know if it's my fault that those can only hold a pretty small amount of weight. I don't know how I feel about taking the blame on that one."

The ghost hovered, but a little lower to the ground. Closer to me. It was working. Just had to keep laying on the ol' charm.

"Um, one time I also got my head stuck in a bucket. You know, if you look at buckets, the yellow ones that roll on the floor and have a picture of a little kid falling in headfirst, that picture is because of me!"

The ghost made a motion that made me think it was laughing at me. Which is when I pulled out my pistol.

This isn't a lesson they teach you in ghost hunting school. This is all me. You're welcome. You're welcome in advance.

Carry a pistol. Like a really huge handgun, a scary one. The one I got, I know it's scary and huge because it was on sale when I bought it, and the reason it was on sale is because the gun store guy said the barrel is too long and it gets caught on holsters when people pull it out. "Impractical" is what he called my Roseanne, which is what I call my pistol.

Bring a gun when you're doing an investigation. Because if you suspect that a ghost is a fake, pointing a gun is a real quick way to figure it out for sure.

I pulled out Roseanne (sometimes I call her "Rosie" if I'm feeling affectionate) and pointed her at the ghost.

The ghost didn't move. So I pulled back the hammer and waited. The ghost still sat there, and then we were doing what's called a Mexican standoff. I'm not sure what's Mexican about it, but that's what most people seem to call it.

Then I decided I'd had enough stand-offing and fired.

I'll be the first to admit, a pistol firing in a closed bathroom is loud as hell. You can't hear much of anything after. Which is good because when you fire off a pistol in an abandoned warehouse, people ask you a lot of annoying questions about why you did that and don't ever do that again, but if your ears are making this hum noise you can't really hear anything and it's really easy to ignore everybody else. Plus, it's impossible for their voices to replay in your head the next time you shoot at a ghost.

You learn nothing is what I'm saying. The big advantage of shooting a loud gun inside a bathroom is you don't have to learn.

After I fired, the ghost disappeared. Which makes me pretty sure that it was a real ghost and not a faker. You might think I'd also be sure because I shot the ghost and it didn't get hurt, but I'm almost positive I missed the ghost. I'm a really bad shot. Like really bad. There was some busted tile on the wall sort of behind where the ghost was, but not really.

But let's not talk about how bad I am with a pistol right now. Let's just focus on the ghost disappearing and how that probably meant it was a real ghost.

You might think a bunch of people would run into the bathroom when they heard the shot. But it was the opposite. Most paranormal investigators, or most paranormal investigation students, anyway, they run like hell when there's a real crime going on. Sure, if you can find a ghost of a little girl who got pushed down a well in 1742, then by all means, figure out whodunit, dig up that asshole's corpse, kick it in the crotch, and move on. But if you're ever in a real crime, don't expect a paranormalist to come help you. Bunch of cowards.

I was alone in the bathroom, and when I left there was nobody anywhere in the building either. I had to go back outside by the van before I found everyone. They were all pretending like they were done investigating when really it was the gunshot that scared them off. I tried to pretend too, but it was hard because I couldn't hear a damn thing.

Someone said, "Get any good ghost audio in there," I think. Because I tried to read his lips.

I said, "Yeah, totally." back, and his face made it pretty clear that he asked something different than what I thought. Also, his face made it clear that I couldn't read lips. I also couldn't read most other things like newspapers. Even billboards were hard for me sometimes, unless they had the same short word a bunch of times, like "Girls, girls, girls."

In class the next day we all sat around and played the tapes we recorded. They were mostly pretty bad, so I was excited to get to mine because I knew I'd seen a ghost. There was a tape where someone was just knocking shit over far away, and then there was another one where a lady was whispering into the microphone about how she was sure the temperature just dropped about 10 degrees, which nobody cared about because she's always freezing in class and asking everyone else if they're cold and why they're not cold.

When it was my turn, I stepped up to the table at the front of the class, hooked up my recorder to the speaker system and pressed PLAY.

The sounds from the ghost encounter were not as good as I remembered. I remembered hearing that sound, that song that goes "Duh-nuh-nuh….nuh-nuh-nuh-nuuuuh-nuh." You know, the one that sounds like boring classical music but it's really the song they play when Dracula shows up. But I guess that didn't really happen.

Then I had to explain my typewriter peeing thing. That was harder to explain than it was to do, and it was pretty hard to do.

Finally, when I was telling the stories to the ghost, everyone started laughing and I said that I never told the ghost that stuff, and it was probably some kind of spectral distortion. That's a term I used. I saw it in one of our textbooks one time. Those books have tons of good stuff like that in there, you just have to take the time to read them. Or, maybe not read them, but read the words that are in dark, black, bigger letters. We get it, textbooks. You could make those things a lot shorter if you just took all the stuff in big black thick letters and then got rid of the rest of the stuff in there. It's like textbooks are trying to prove how smart they are. We KNOW, okay? I don't care how you learned something or how you know it. Just tell me the something you know and let's move on.

Anyway, I think most of the class bought it because one of the dirty secrets of paranormal investigation school is that nobody reads the textbooks. If we were good at reading textbooks, we'd get legitimate degrees and then real jobs. Besides, when have you seen someone investigating something with a big ass book? Never.

I was at my office, and my ear was bleeding. I was digging ear wax out with my keys, and usually when I do that I stop as soon as I hit something and hear this sort of high pitched whining sound. But this time I already had that sound in my head from when I shot off that gun in the bathroom, so I had to dig in deeper until I got some other sign that told me I'd gone in far enough. In this case, blood was a pretty good substitute.

I had just felt a drop of blood hit my shoulder when the dame walked in. This time it was the guy kind of dame, but whatever, they're all dames when you're a detective.

The guy sat at my table, and he held out a business card.

"Is this you?" he said.

It was my card. I could tell right away because the card he held wasn't mine, but it was for the real estate place I steal stacks of cards from all the time. They just throw them out when they get new agents, which is like every day, so then I take them and use the backs. Did you know most business cards are blank on the back? Wasteful. No wonder people have such a hard time staying in business.

I said, "That's me. What can I do for a dame like you?"

He mostly ignored what I said, and he said, "Your ear is bleeding."

And I said, "Yeah. Old ghost hunting wound."

He said, "I've got a problem."

After that he talked for a really long time. I find it's best to let people tell you their entire problem, the whole story from the beginning, and what you do is not listen and then make them do it a second time. That way you get the quick version. I learned this trick from the doctor when I had to explain like ten times why I had key scrapes in my ears that wouldn't heal.

When he finished, I said, "So you think you've got a...little girl in a well kind of thing?"

He stopped. He was looking at my shoulder, and I did too. There was a pretty good amount of blood on my shirt. I thought it had stopped because I didn't feel the drips anymore, but instead of stopping what really happened is that it went to a steady stream, which was hitting my shoulder.

"Uh, no," he said, "It's a haunted doll."

Haunted dolls are total bread and butter. I don't know what it is about dolls, but they freak people the fuck out.

Maybe it's because of the uncanny valley.

...

I'm going to admit to you right now that I have no idea what the uncanny valley is. It's just something I heard someone say in class before. But I DID think it would be a really good name for a strip club. Especially if the people you hired to strip had unusual butt cracks. Like really long ones or wide ones or butt cracks that were jagged, maybe like a lightning bolt.

Sideways ass crack would obviously be the crown jewel. But that's gotta be hard to come by, and frankly I think someone who's stripping and has a sideways butt crack can probably make plenty of money on her own. What does she need with the Uncanny Valley (LLC)?

Anyway, there's something about dolls that just puts people off. Which is why they're a great moneymaker for guys like me.

I went with the guy to his house. Or what I thought was his house until I saw the yard. There was all this shit in it. Like you know that thing where it's a bird bath, but instead of the water dish on top, it's a glass ball with a mirrored outside? This guy's yard had one of those. And you know those things where it's a cutout of an old man and an old woman, and they're bending over to do yard work and you can see their underwear? Those were there too.

Birdhouses, hummingbird feeders. All kinds of shit.

I decided to ask the question that was rolling around in my mind. It's always good to get more information from someone when you're doing an investigation. It was just a matter of asking it delicately.

"What's with all the shit in your yard?" I said.

I couldn't think of a delicate way to ask. Besides, delicate isn't for hauntings. It's for that setting on the washing machine that nobody uses because, duh, what are you putting in there, dinner plates?

The guy said, "It's not my shit. Well, it's my shit. Sort of. We just bought the house, and it came with all the stuff that was in there before."

"Like the haunted doll?" I said.

"Like the doll," he said.

"Show me."

The house had one of those attics where you pull a little rope and then stairs come shooting down out of the attic. Totally awesome. I have to say, if I was a haunted doll, that's where I would be too.

We went up the stairs, and the guy shushed me. Probably because I was talking really loud, but maybe because I was talking really loud about how Burger King changed their coffee lids and they're better for drinking, but not very good when you're on a stakeout and you have to pee in the cup.

The guy pointed, and off to the side, in this perfect sunbeam of light through a little window, there was a tiny rocking chair.

And in that chair was the doll.

We snuck back down, and I laced up my stompin'
boots, which I told the guy were magic boots that kept me
anchored in this plane, and I went upstairs.

Your creepy dolls come in a couple varieties, but for the most
part, they're more alike than they are different.

For one thing, they're ALWAYS a soul trapped in a doll,
not just some doll that's always been alive. That's stupid.

Two, they're ALWAYS evil. Or evil-ish. The point being,
I've never encountered a possessed doll where the guy got
inside a doll's body to help people. You know that story about
the goblins or whatever who help that one dude cobble shoes
(whatever the hell that is)? Bullshit. Nothing supernatural is
good. And nothing supernatural is looking for a goddamn job.
They don't even have to eat! What do they need a job for?

Now, your main differences are you've got your:

Vintage Dolls: This is a way of saying "really old doll" but in a
way where the doll is worth more money. These are usually

some kid who grew up in a creepy mansion that burned down. These dolls are pretty easy to deal with. Usually you can show them what Netflix is, their minds are blown, and you're done. Or, alternative, you can just stomp the shit out of them with your stompin' boots.

Modern Dolls: These are usually inhabited by a deranged killer who jumped into the doll's body at the last second before death. Why he would do that only when dying is a mystery to me. And why wouldn't you go into, I don't know, the Predator statue they always have at Sharper Image? Or a car or something? Wait, that's a Stephen King story. Okay, some kind of industrial machine? Shit, that's King too. That guy's thought of everything.

I find the best way to deal with these dolls is a good ol' fashioned stompin'.

Action Figures: First of all, don't call these dolls. They get really pissed off when you call them dolls, and they always have to tell you the difference between dolls and action figures. Something about articulation. I don't know. I don't usually listen because I pretty much can smash any action figure with one good stomp, so they don't get to say much, especially if they start out by correcting me.

I crept up on the doll in the chair as quietly as I could. Which wasn't very quiet because I was wearing the stompin' boots (remember!?), and when you have stompin' boots on, your feet just kind of want to start stompin' right away, even if you're not anywhere near whatever needs stompin' and whatever needs stompin' is still in a chair instead of being on the ground and being like, "No, no, no! I'm an extraordinary creature! Please don't stomp meeeee!"

When I got close (kind of) the doll whipped around in the chair.

It was one of those dummies that people use to talk. I've never stomped one of them before, but it looked like it was painstakingly handcrafted, and man I couldn't wait to get to stompin.

Too bad for me, he stood up, and he started to talk.

"So," he said, "I see my little revenge plot is—"

And then I started a-stompin'.

Here's another tip if you're getting into the ghost business. Don't listen. Ghosts never have anything to say. Or if they do, it's about how you could stop them if only you'd gotten some amulet or blah blah blah. Meanwhile, if you just stomp 'em, you can be home in time for dinner. If you have a home and dinner. Must be nice.

I crushed part of the dummy's torso, but then he rolled over and got away from me.

He ran over to where there was this knife block with all the knives in it. I thought I was in big trouble, but he tried to grab one, and he couldn't bend his hand or his fingers, so his hand slipped right over the handle. Then he went for another one, but then that one was too big.

I figured I'd better stop him before he did enough experimenting to find a knife that fit into the current position of his fingers, so I charged forward and then booted him across the attic.

He smashed into this open footlocker, and when he hit the lid he fell inside and the lid closed on top of him. I ran over really quick and put this big bust of Shakespeare on top of it to hold it down. Was it Shakespeare? Was Shakespeare the guy who wrote the "Duh nuh nuh nuh!" song, or was Shakespeare the guy who wore one of those circle air filters around his neck?

Well, whoever he was, he was enough to hold down the doll.

With the bust on top, I decided to do a seance and remove the evil spirit. By which I mean, light the fucking footlocker on fire, burn that bastard down.

I had my seance kit (matches, oily rags (which I normally call "my socks")) and I started to get the seance ready when the dummy started talking.

"Hey, whoa. I don't know what you're doing out there, but it smells like a garbage fire."

I said, "It only smells like garbage because it's my socks. But don't you worry, the fire part is coming."

He said, "Hold up. You don't wanna do that. There's some magazines in here."

"What do I care about magazines?" I said.

He said, " Not just any magazines. Pornographic ones. Good, late-70's stuff too."

I don't know how he knew that I liked late-70's porno. Probably because he had powers. Maybe because everybody who's ever given it some thought likes late-70's porno. That doesn't really matter. What matters is that I decided to take Shakespeare off the lid and open up the footlocker, just enough for the doll to slide some of the porno out.

I said, "Show me one of the magazines. Then we'll talk."

The dummy banged against the top of the footlocker. He tried to throw the lid open, but he wasn't very strong. This is something that us ghost hunter types never tell you about possessed dolls. They're super weak and shitty. Think about it, if a doll came to life, do you think it could bench press...however much it is that's a lot to bench press? No way. They'd be about as strong as what they are, a little kid who has no bones and is made out of plastic. Hell, half of them are babies!

I said, "You're not getting out of there. You might as well hand me the porno."

The lid was open wide enough that the dummy could slide his arms out, and he got them wedged, then got his head out. But I closed the lid on his neck and put the Shakespeare statue on top.

I figured it was a good time to come up with an action movie line. "Like Shakespare said," and I pointed at the bust, "Case. Closed."

The dummy spun its head around on its neck. Again, that would be terrifying if it had a spine. And then he said, "First of all, no. Shakespeare never said that."

I was about to jump right on the footlocker lid and decapitate that fucker, but then I stopped. This guy knew a lot. Maybe he could be useful. But then I thought what could also be useful would be for me to decapitate that fucker. Useful because I would feel a lot better about it.

Cut to a few hours later, I'm at the Burger King, and the dummy's head is on the table across from me.

It turns out possessed dummy heads can still talk and think and all that stuff without their bodies. They're powered by magic anyway, so I guess they don't need lungs and shit. Or they never had any to begin with. I don't think most dummies are built with guts and stuff inside. That seems wasteful, and it kind of seems like it's inviting trouble too.

The dummy went on and on about how I didn't need to burn its body, and that I definitely didn't need to pee out the flames, but I felt it was a matter of professionalism. I do my job, and I do it all the way. Sorry.

He was pouting, and he kept saying bad stuff was going to happen. He said, "A zombie plague will be unleashed upon this world."

I said, "Not really interested in zombies. They're kind of played out. Pass."

Then he said, "Vampires. Once again, vampires will roam the—"

"Pass," I said. "Vampires have been fucked out since forever."

The dummy moved its eyes around. Maybe I should have taken the eyes out. They make this weird scraping noise in the sockets, and if I took them out, he'd probably still be able to see. No, wait. No eyes is scarier.

He said, "How about a blob? I know about a blob that's pretty evil."

A blob? Now that's interesting. Everyone's fought a ghost. Mummies are a total danger zone, what with cultural appropriation and everything. Don't fight a mummy anywhere near a college campus unless you want to end up on the business end of a protest with a lot of signs that are pretty stupid but one or two that sting.

But a blob. Now that's intriguing.

I said, "Okay. Show me the blob."

The dummy said, "No. First you have to give me a body."

I said, "No deal." I knew that anything he did with that body would be my responsibility. Legally. And if I had to go back to court AGAIN and yell at a dummy that was just sitting on the witness stand and not moving, playing a really great joke on me and making me look like an idiot, and then I start yelling so much that someone comes in and injects me with something in the neck and I wake up in a different county, well, fool me twice.

After some negotiation we came up with a compromise. Which is why I was pushing around a baby stroller with a legless dummy that had a new torso and arms attached. I figured it was better to give him arms instead of legs. That way he couldn't make a break for it.

The downside was that I had to push around this stroller with what appeared to be either a mutilated dummy or a foul-mouthed baby inside, depending on whether you caught me arguing with the dummy when you walked past.

There's a lot of scary stuff out there, but nothing is scarier than the judgment of other parents.

No, wait. Ghosts are a lot scarier. And blobs. We're getting to that.

The dummy pointed to the wall. "There," he said. "In there."

I walked up to the wall and put my ear up to it. "I don't hear anything," I said.

"Asshole," he said, "I mean that sewer opening." He pointed again, but it still looked like he was pointing straight at the wall. He said, "Maybe if you'd given me some arms with more than just shoulder articulation this would be easier."

I looked at the sewer lid, and I said, "Okay, but if I'm going down there, you're going with me."

"Fine," he said.

"I'm serious. If this is a trick to get me all messed up, then I'm gonna be really pissed."

"That's fine," he said. "It's not a trick."

I stared at him, and he stared back. Or didn't blink. The doll head didn't have the kind of eyes that blink, so it was hard to tell when the dummy head was staring me down or just sort of spaced out. He spaced out a lot, I think.

Something I learned about the human body right then is how bad it is to strain really hard in your gut when you try and lift something heavy. Which is something I learned because I tried to lift the sewer lid off the sewer opening, and holy shit was it heavy. I lifted and strained with all my muscles, just like I learned in gym class where the coach said the way to get strong is you should pull on things until it feels like you're turning inside out. Looking back, he might not have been the best gym coach. He might not have even been legally allowed to work with kids. I've never seen someone other than him who had two ankle monitors on the same leg.

I was laying on the street, breathing hard as hell, and I hadn't moved the sewer lid at all.

"How do you know the blob's down there?" I said.

The dummy said, "Because I seen him come out. Through the holes in the lid."

That gave me an idea.

We bought a bunch of snacks from the corner store. I didn't know what a blob would like, so I figured that we should just get snacks I liked because that way whatever the blob didn't eat I could just eat later. That's why I got Doritos. They don't fit in a sewer all that great, but man are they tasty. I polished off the bag and dumped the crumbs on my face. I didn't mean to dump the crumbs on my face. I meant to dump them in my mouth. But life isn't always about what you want as much as it's about what you end up doing just because that's what happens. Nobody WANTS to wake up covered in urine and melted chocolate with a fistful of candy wrappers in both hands. But then it happens and you learn real quick that what you want isn't always what you get.

I opened the juice bag and fished out the pickles, then tied my bootlaces around the pickle, and then tried to squeeze it into one of the holes on the sewer lid.

We tried the giant pickle next. I like pickles most of the time, but the way they sell them at the gas station is disgusting. In a bag of juice? Like the bag of pickle juice is some kind of great bonus? And the bag of juice had this pickle drawing on it, and the pickle had this lipstick and high heels on, and it sort of looked like a hooker pickle.

I opened the juice bag and fished out the pickles, then tied my bootlaces around the pickle, and then tried to squeeze it into one of the holes on the sewer lid.

The pickle was too big to fit in the hole, but lucky for me I was still wearing my stompin' boots. They'd do the trick. I made sure to turn the dummy in the stroller so he could watch me stomp the pickle like I stomped him. It only took a couple good stomps before the pickle fell through the hole and into the sewer.

After that, it was the waiting game. Which is what I usually call Scrabble because you can win that game if you just take so long to make moves that everyone else quits.

I tied the bootlace around my finger, and we waited.

We didn't wait long. I did have to pee once, probably because I drank that whole bag of pickle juice. I just peed straight in one of the sewer lid holes. That probably saves water, right? No flush? Straight to the source?

Anyway, we didn't have to wait long before there was a tug on the string. And then a bigger tug. And then all this pink slime started pouring out from the holes in the sewer lid.

The blob spread out in the alley and rose up to full size. I guess. Sometimes it seems like the blob grows and shrinks. I think that's impossible. But also I think it's a blob, so maybe it doesn't have the same rules. In fact, I KNOW it doesn't have the same rules because I can't fit my body through a hole in a sewer lid. I can't even fit my body through a small waterslide. But that's mostly a fear thing. Partially it's obesity rampaging my body, but it's mostly a fear thing.

Full size or not, the blob was pretty big. Big enough to block out the sun. Except you can see through the blob, so you could still see the sun. Whatever. Really big is what I mean.

I made a run for it. The dummy, stuck in the stroller, was screaming at me, something about how I was the real dummy and come pick him up and other stuff like that. But I ignored him. Because fuck that guy.

In fact, fuck that guy so hard that I got around the corner, then peered out to watch the blob destroy him.

The blob leaned down into the stroller. The dummy screamed some more stuff. The blob stopped. It leaned back again, and it tilted its head. Or, I don't know. It's really hard to describe what a blob is doing. It doesn't have parts. It blobs around. But it sort of moved around in a way that made me think the blob was listening.

Then the blob leaned into the stroller, sucked up the dummy, and stood back up again.

Which was pretty awesome until the dummy's body floated to the top, and its head poked out the top of the blob, and then the dummy was controlling the blob.

Probably the worst thing you can do, as a ghost investigator guy, is to combine two pretty bad ghosts into one ghost that's even worse. Partly because you've unleashed a terror on the world, but partly because if those ghosts are both mad at you, then you're their number one target.

I made a run for it. Then a walk for it. Then I made a lean up against the side of a building for it.

The blob poked its dummy head around the corner, and it said, "Ah ha! Got you now!" and it reached out a slimy tendril and wrapped it around my face. I was doomed.

Okay, I wasn't doomed. But I thought I was for a couple seconds. Long enough to put that section break in there, make you feel like how I felt.

What happened is sewage saved my life.

The blob spent so much time in the sewer that it took on the sewage stink. And when it wrapped its thing around my face, the first thing I did was hurl. A lot. I'd eaten a lot of chicken rods at the office that day.

The hurl ate through the blob's slime, and it dropped me on the sidewalk. I broke the fall with my front teeth, which are the breakaway panels evolution put there to absorb hard blows to the face, and I got to my feet.

I held one of my teeth in my mouth, deciding to swallow it for safekeeping or spit it into my hand, when the blob made a fist and punched me in the stomach, and I spit out the tooth into the gutter. The punch hurt like hell, but at least I didn't have to make the decision about the tooth anymore. Sometimes things work out like that. You can't decide if you should get a new TV or not, and then your homemade microwave breaks down, lights your place on fire, and then you really have no choice.

The blob turned its fist into a hand, and it looked just like one of those sticky hands you buy for a quarter at the grocery store, the ones that come in those plastic eggs. As it was slapping me hard across the face, I got an idea. Then the idea got slapped out of my face, but then a couple more slaps, and it was back, baby.

I grinned, and the dummy saw my messed up teeth and the blob body dropped me. Just long enough to scuttle across the street to the cat rescue.

See, here's what I remembered. I remembered that what messed up those sticky hands, more than anything, was cat hair. You dropped the sticky hand on the carpet, it got covered in cat hair, and the fantasy was over. You thought you were going to be like the kid on the picture inside the egg machine, the picture where the kid was snatching a dollar bill off the ground? You thought you were going to snatch a dollar, then be smart and buy four more sticky hands, and then each sticky hand would snatch up another dollar, and pretty soon you'd be walking down the street, snatching up all the money that's always laying around like some kind of money-grabbing double octopus with colorful, sticky hands? But one clumsy moment over a carpet covered in cat hair, that's all it took to destroy my dreams.

Inside the cat rescue, things were a little disorganized. Probably because on the street outside a blob with a dummy's head was smashing up a hot dog cart like crazy.

I said, "Excuse me. I'd like to adopt your cats."

Someone ducked behind the counter said, "Which one?"

I said, "All of them."

The person said, "No. That's crazy."

I said, "Maybe this rod will convince you otherwise."

I don't know if the person behind the counter thought I meant "gun" when I said "rod," or maybe they thought I was talking about my wiener. What I was really talking about was a chicken rod I had in my wallet. I wanted to offer a bribe, but all that I found in there was a folded up, mashed chicken rod I was saving for later.

Either way, they gave me the keys to one of the rooms down the hall, and I ran in to get some cats.

The room I got the keys for must have been the room of last chances. Because there were a bunch of old, smelly cats in there.

Old cats are just like old people. Everybody thinks it's sad they're homeless, but nobody wants to take them in. I can pee all over the floor myself just fine, thanks.

I grabbed up as many cats as I could carry. Which is one. All the other ones I tried to pick up scratched my like crazy. I should've known. You don't live to be an old cat unless you know how to scratch someone like me. Unless you learn that lesson early and often, you'll never make it.

The one I got was hairy, though. And sleepy. He only opened one eye a little bit when I took him outside, and then he shut it again. The look in his eye told me everything, that he was totally planning to scratch the hell out of me later, but for now, more naps.

I burst out of the door, and the dummy blob was standing there with almost a whole car inside it.

I held the cat in one hand, like a football, and I knew this was it. This is when I needed the line.

I tried to think of something with pussy. Then something about cat scratch fever. Then something about dander or hair or something.

Someone on the street screamed, "Oh my god. You're not going to throw that cat are you?"

I looked exactly like I was going to throw that cat. Like I was a football trophy come to life, except no athleticism and the football was a sleepy cat.

I thought about what I was doing. This was my own mess. Not this poor cat's. I should be the one to sacrifice. To clean it up.

But then I thought about something else, which is that I was about to be a hero. If this plan worked, I'd be like that football guy who gets the trophy. Only better because I didn't just win some stupid game where they pass a ball to each other through their legs and under their nutsack.

I threw the cat. Straight into the blob.

The effect was immediate. The blob kind of fell over. Then turned into a flat chunk of slime. It wasn't sticky anymore. It was just...fuzzy. And gross.

The dummy head was yelling, cursing and saying something in another language that sounded evil. I did what I should have done in the first place and stomped him to pieces.

Then I went to check on the cat.

The cat was dead. I was pretty sure. Or dying. It made this weird noise, and I pulled out trusty Roseanne from her holser to finish him off and do the right thing, and that's when I got tackled by a bunch of people who were standing around. I guess they were too cool to help with the blob, but stopping me from putting a cat out of its misery, THAT was up their alley.

There's one last thing I have to teach you about being a ghost detective.

Society isn't ready for ghost detectives. Not yet. They just want to show the news clip of you trying to shoot an old, sleepy cat. Who wasn't dying, by the way. The sound I thought was a dying sound was a meow. Old cats make fucked up noises.

But what I will admit is that when I watched the news clip, Roseanne's size next to the cat made me look pretty insane. I would've tackled me too.

The bad side of all this is that the clip on the news and having a giant handgun will get you kicked right out of your Burger KIng office. Well, not just the clip and the gun, but also because the manager just loses it and tells you not to call them chicken rods, but you do it again anyway, and the guy shoves you out into the bushes, where there's a passed-out guy already taking up most of the bush, so you kind of fall on him, and the worst part is, he wakes up, and you can tell he's mad, but he sees you got kicked out and your clothes are covered in slime and cat hair, and you smell like a sewer, and also you smile at him and don't have any teeth in the front.

And this bum, he pats you on the arm, and he's like, "You okay, buddy?"

Some people would call that rock bottom. But I call it air top. Or top rock. Or whatever the opposite of rock bottom is. Because the good news is that I solved a real case. And I can get my ghost detective license now. My real one. Right after I write this all up and send it off to the dean of the ghost school. Who has a really cool website with a black background and bright green writing all over it. And who I hope will give me a diploma. And who is probably really handsome and great.

Printed in Great Britain
by Amazon

86564337R00039